This book is comprised of s
meeting serial killers. This i
not represent any actual true events. All stories in this book
are for entertainment purposes only.

"Stay endlessly curious, because wonder is where growth begins. And never forget—this is *your* life to live, not a script to follow. Be bold enough to ask your own questions, and brave enough to write your own answers."

-Amanda Fisher

"Charlie"

The desert air hung heavy, thick with the scent of Joshua trees and paranoia. The year was 1968. I was a lost sheep, barely 18, hitchhiking across California, chasing a freedom I couldn't define. I'd been dropped off on the edge of Death Valley, the sun a malevolent eye in the sky, when a beat-up VW bus, painted with swirling, faded flowers, pulled over.

"Need a ride, sister?" a voice crackled from the driver's seat.

Inside, the air was thick with incense and something else, something earthy and unsettling. A scruffy-bearded man with piercing, unsettling eyes sat in the driver's seat. He introduced himself as Charlie. He had an unsettling aura, a magnetic pull coupled with a disquieting stillness. He wore a stained white t-shirt and a pair of faded jeans that looked older than me.

"We're headed up to Spahn Ranch," he said, a smile that didn't quite reach his eyes playing on his lips. "Got room for one more."

Spahn Ranch. I'd heard whispers of it. A remote movie set, now a commune, a place for free spirits and lost souls. It sounded like exactly what I was looking for. Hesitantly, I climbed in.

The bus was crammed with young women, all with long, tangled hair and sun-kissed skin. They introduced themselves with names like Squeaky, Gypsy, and Sadie. They were friendly, almost unnaturally so, their eyes holding a glazed look that I couldn't quite decipher. They sang songs as we bumped along the dusty road, songs I'd never heard before, filled with cryptic lyrics about revolution and rebirth.

When we arrived at the ranch, the sun was beginning its fiery descent. The place was a shambles of dilapidated buildings and overgrown brush. But there was a certain beauty to the decay, a sense of wild abandonment.

Charlie, as he was called, was immediately surrounded. He was like a messiah to these people, a guru, a god. He dispensed hugs and pronouncements with the same casual ease. He greeted me with a warm smile and a hand on my shoulder.

"Welcome home," he said, his eyes boring into mine.

That night, around a crackling bonfire, he spoke. He spoke of the coming apocalypse, of a race war that would cleanse the earth, of a new Eden that would rise from the ashes. He spoke with a fervor that was both captivating and terrifying. The others listened with rapt attention, their eyes shining with a fervent belief.

I sat on the periphery, unnerved. There was something deeply wrong, something rotten at the core of this idyllic facade. His words, though couched in love and peace, hinted at something violent, something dangerous.

I saw him then, in the flickering firelight, not as a charismatic leader, but as a predator, a spider weaving a web of delusion. He was a master manipulator, preying on the vulnerable, the lost, the seeking.

Later, as the others slept beneath the stars, I couldn't. I lay awake, listening to the desert night, the coyote howls echoing my own unease. I knew I had to leave.

The next morning, I slipped away before dawn. I didn't say goodbye, didn't leave a note. I just walked. I walked for miles, until I found a highway, a lifeline back to the world I knew, the world I was running from, but suddenly yearned for.

I never told anyone about my night at Spahn Ranch. The memory remained a dark secret, a stain on my soul. It wasn't until years later, when the Manson Family's crimes were splashed across the headlines, that I understood the true horror I had escaped.

The night I met Charles Manson wasn't just a night; it was a brush with pure evil, a stark reminder of the darkness that lurks beneath the surface of even the most beautiful illusions. It was a night that changed me, forever shaping my perception of the world and the people who inhabit it. And it was a night I will never, ever forget.

"The Charm Killer"

The chipped ceramic mug warmed my hands as I stared out the rain-streaked window of "The Bean Scene." Seattle was living up to its reputation. I was nursing a lukewarm latte and trying to outline my criminology paper, a topic ironically about the psychology of serial killers. Ironic because, at that moment, they felt more like abstract monsters from a textbook than real people.

The bell above the door jingled, breaking my concentration. A man walked in, shaking the rain from his dark wool coat. He was strikingly handsome, with a captivating smile that seemed genuine and warm, even in the dreary lighting. He caught my eye and offered a quick, friendly nod.

I instinctively nodded back. He ordered a coffee from the barista and then turned, scanning the room. It wasn't crowded; a couple huddled in a booth, a lone student hunched over a textbook, and me. He walked towards the empty chair opposite my table.

"Mind if I join you?" he asked, his voice smooth and pleasant. "Every other seat seems to be taken."

"Of course," I said, feeling a sudden, inexplicable nervousness. "Go ahead."

He settled into the chair, placing his coffee carefully on the table. "Ted," he said, extending his hand. "Ted Bundy."

My mind stuttered. Bundy… The name echoed in my head. I'd been reading about him, researching him. This had to be a coincidence, a very unsettling coincidence.

"Sarah," I replied, shaking his hand. His grip was firm, confident.

We talked for a while. About the weather, about Seattle, about the terrible coffee at The Bean Scene. He was charming, articulate, and surprisingly... normal. He asked about my books, and I told him about my criminology studies, carefully avoiding the subject of serial killers altogether.

"So, you're interested in understanding the criminal mind?" he asked, his eyes seeming to bore into mine. There was a subtle shift in his demeanor, a flicker that I couldn't quite decipher.

"It's fascinating," I said, choosing my words carefully. "Trying to understand what drives people to do unspeakable things."

He leaned back in his chair, a thoughtful expression on his face. "I think a lot of it comes down to feeling powerless," he said. "Feeling like the world has dealt you a bad hand, and wanting to take back control."

His words hung in the air, heavier than they should have been. It was a common theory, one I'd read about in countless books. But coming from him, from someone with that name, the analysis felt unnervingly acute.

The rain outside intensified, drumming against the windowpane. The coffee shop seemed to shrink around us, the other patrons fading into a blurry background.

"Have you ever felt that way, Sarah?" he asked, his voice low and intense. "Powerless?"

I hesitated, caught off guard by the personal question. "Everyone feels powerless sometimes, I guess."

He smiled, a smile that didn't quite reach his eyes. "It's how you deal with that feeling that matters, isn't it?"

We continued to talk, but the atmosphere had shifted subtly. I was acutely aware of his presence, of the weight of his words, of the unsettling coincidence that had brought us together. I couldn't shake the feeling that I was being studied, analyzed.

Eventually, he glanced at his watch. "I should be going," he said. "It was lovely talking to you, Sarah."

He stood up, and for a moment, I felt a rush of relief. The encounter had been unnerving, unsettling. But then, he paused.

"You know," he said, leaning closer, his voice a low whisper, "sometimes, the monsters we fear are the people we least expect."

He smiled, a chillingly charming smile, and then turned and walked out into the rain.

I sat there for a long time after he left, the chipped ceramic mug cold in my hands. The rain had stopped, and a weak ray of sunshine peeked through the clouds. But the coffee shop felt darker than before, the air thick with a lingering unease.

I looked down at my criminology paper, the words blurring on the page. The monsters I thought I only knew from textbooks had suddenly become terrifyingly real. I had just met Ted Bundy, and the chilling conversation had left me with a profound sense of disquiet, questioning everything I thought I knew about the nature of evil. Was it something born, or something made? And was it possible to look into the eyes of a monster and not see… a monster? The questions swirled in my head, unanswered, leaving me cold in the Seattle sunshine.

"The Milwaukee Monster"

The stench of bleach and something sickly sweet clung to the air, a cloying combination that threatened to choke the back of my throat. My head throbbed. I blinked, the dim light of the room doing little to ease the disorientation. Where was I? More importantly, *how* did I get here?

Fragments flickered: a bar, a conversation, a friendly face. Too friendly, maybe. And then...nothing.

Panic clawed at my insides. I was tied to a rickety chair, the coarse rope biting into my wrists. The room was small, sparsely furnished with a stained mattress and a single, flickering bulb overhead. A cluttered shelf held an assortment of tools – hammers, saws, things that glinted ominously in the weak light.

Then I saw him.

He stood in the doorway, a figure cast in shadow. Jeffrey. I remembered his name from the bar, his easy smile. But the smile was gone now, replaced by something unsettling, something dead behind the eyes.

"You're awake," he said, his voice flat, devoid of emotion.

My heart hammered against my ribs. I knew, instinctively, that I was in terrible danger. This wasn't a robbery gone wrong. This was something far, far worse.

He moved closer, and the details of his face sharpened. His eyes were...empty. He picked up a syringe from the shelf.

That's when the primal scream building within me finally broke free. I thrashed against the ropes, yelling, pleading, begging him to let me go.

He flinched, the syringe momentarily forgotten. My struggles, desperate and fueled by pure terror, had loosened the ropes a fraction. A tiny fraction, but enough.

I kept screaming, thrashing. He lunged, trying to subdue me, and in that moment, I saw my chance. With a surge of adrenaline, I wrenched my hands against the rope again, ignoring the burning pain. The frayed fibers finally gave way.

My hands were free.

I scrambled to my feet, knocking the chair over with a clang. He was faster than I expected, but I was driven by the sheer will to survive. I kicked him, catching him off balance, and bolted for the door.

He roared, a sound that chased me down the narrow hallway. I didn't look back. I slammed the door open and burst out into the night.

The air was cold, crisp, blessedly clean. I ran. I ran until my lungs burned, until my legs screamed, until I collapsed, gasping, behind a dumpster in a dark alley.

Later, huddled in the shadows, I tried to make sense of what had happened. The police... I should go to the police. But the thought terrified me. What would I say? How could I explain? The shame, the humiliation... and the fear. What if they didn't believe me? What if he came looking for me again?

He knew my name. He knew what I looked like.

The fear was a cold knot in my stomach. Reporting him felt like inviting him back into my life, risking everything all over again.

So, I made a choice. A cowardly choice, perhaps. I ran. I ran as far as I could, changed my name, got a new identity. I became someone else, someone unrecognizable.

I carried the secret with me, a dark, festering wound. The nightmares came, vivid and terrifying. The guilt gnawed at me. What if he did this to someone else? What if, by my silence, I had condemned another victim to a fate I had narrowly escaped?

Years passed. I saw the news reports, the grisly details, the arrest. Relief washed over me, followed by a renewed wave of guilt. He was caught, but I still hadn't done the right thing. I had prioritized my own safety over justice, over the potential lives that could have been saved.

The truth was a burden I would carry forever. I lived in the shadows, haunted by the memory of the man in the doorway and the weight of my own silence. I was free, but I was also a prisoner. A prisoner of my own fear, and the terrible secret I could never truly escape.

"Pogo the Clown"

The balloons were a sickly sweet pink, the kind that made your teeth ache just looking at them. I didn't care. I was five, and pink was my favorite colour. My backyard, usually just a patch of grass and a tired swing set, was transformed. Streamers crisscrossed the fence, a bouncy castle pulsed with excited children, and the air crackled with the sugary promise of cake.

The main event, though, hadn't arrived yet. My parents had promised a clown, and I was practically vibrating with anticipation. I loved clowns. Their painted smiles, their silly walks, their boundless energy – it was all magic to me.

Then, he arrived. A beat-up rusty pickup truck lurched to a stop at the curb, and out stepped Pogo. His face was painted in a classic white mask, thick red lips stretching into a wide, seemingly genuine smile. Blue triangles sat above his eyes, adding a touch of whimsy. He wore a baggy rainbow suit that seemed to swallow him whole, and carried a bouquet of brightly coloured balloon animals.

Right away, I was captivated. Pogo wasn't like the clowns in the movies. He was… gentler. His voice was soft, almost a whisper, and his eyes, visible behind the paint, held a surprising warmth. He handed me a balloon dog, carefully constructed and perfectly formed.

He started his act. It wasn't slapstick or pie-in-the-face humor. Instead, he told stories with his body, miming hilarious situations with exaggerated gestures and expressive faces. He made us laugh with silly voices and pulled endless handkerchiefs from his sleeve. He even did a little magic show, making coins disappear and reappear behind our ears.

But the best part was how he interacted with us. He made each of us feel special, asking our names, telling us how smart and funny we were. He didn't just perform; he connected. He knelt down to my level, his painted smile unwavering, and asked me what my favorite part of my birthday had been so far.

"You!" I blurted out, my cheeks flushing pinker than the balloons.

He chuckled, a low, rumbling sound. "Well, I'm glad to hear that, young lady."

The party continued, filled with laughter and games. Pogo remained the center of it all, a gentle giant of colour and cheer. As the sun began to set, casting long shadows across the lawn, it was time for him to go.

He knelt down one last time, pulling me into a gentle hug. "Happy birthday, sweetie," he whispered. "Remember to always smile."

I never forgot Pogo. For years, I told the story of the clown at my fifth birthday, the one who made me laugh and feel like the most important person in the world.

Then, years later, the news broke. The horrifying, unimaginable truth. John Wayne Gacy. And the picture that flashed across the television screen... the picture of Pogo the Clown...

The memory of that day, once so bright and joyful, instantly turned cold and tainted. The warmth in his eyes, the gentle voice, the genuine smile – they all took on a sinister new meaning. The image of him kneeling down, hugging me... it sent shivers down my spine.

The pink balloons, the laughter, the magic... it was all poisoned now. The innocence of my fifth birthday, stolen and corrupted by the horrifying reality of the man behind the painted smile. The joy had been replaced by a chilling understanding: the monster I had unknowingly embraced under the summer sun. My childhood was forever marked, not by a happy memory, but by the terrifying realization that evil can wear a clown suit, and sometimes, it even gives you a balloon dog.

"The Valley Intruder"

The flickering candlelight cast dancing shadows on his face, softening what I later realized were sharp, almost predatory features. He'd introduced himself as Richard, and there was something captivating about the way he held my gaze, a kind of intense focus that made me feel utterly seen. I was immediately drawn in.

We were at a secluded Italian restaurant, the kind with dark wood and heavy drapes, the kind that whispered secrets. Richard had chosen it, said he liked the "old world charm." He was dressed impeccably in a dark suit, his hair slicked back, and his eyes, a deep dark brown, seemed to absorb the dim light.

He was fascinating. He talked about art, about philosophy, about the beauty he found in unusual places. He spoke with a passion that was almost unnerving, like a coiled spring ready to unleash. He told me about his travels, weaving tales of sun-drenched beaches and bustling city streets, but the stories lacked detail, felt… fabricated. I chalked it up to his artistic temperament.

I, on the other hand, was babbling about my mundane life – my job as a librarian, my love for old movies, my cat, Mr. Whiskers. He listened intently, nodding, asking questions that were deceptively simple, yet probed deeper than seemed necessary. He wanted to know where I lived, my work schedule, whether I lived alone. I wasn't alarmed then, just flattered by the attention.

He complimented my perfume, something with vanilla and sandalwood. "It's intoxicating," he murmured, leaning closer. A shiver ran down my spine, a mixture of excitement and unease.

As the evening progressed, his conversation took a darker turn. He spoke of the inherent darkness in people, about the primal urges that lay simmering beneath the surface. He talked about the thrill of the hunt, the power of owning someone. He couched it all in philosophical terms, referring to Nietzsche and the will to power, but the undercurrent was unmistakable.

I started to feel uncomfortable. I excused myself to the restroom, escaping the intensity of his gaze. As I splashed cold water on my face, I couldn't shake the feeling that I was being watched, even in the empty bathroom.

When I returned to the table, he was gone. The waiter informed me he'd paid the bill and left a message. I found a small, folded piece of paper waiting for me. Inside, scrawled in elegant handwriting, was a single line: "See you soon."

That night, I couldn't sleep. Richard's words kept echoing in my mind, his intense eyes burning behind my eyelids. I tried to rationalize my discomfort, telling myself I was being paranoid, that he was just a little… eccentric.

The next morning, I woke up to the blaring of the news. A wave of terror crashed over me as I saw his picture splashed across the screen. Richard Ramirez. The Night Stalker. Wanted in connection with a string of brutal home invasions, rapes, and murders.

My blood ran cold. The pieces clicked into place. The lack of detail in his stories, the unnerving intensity, the probing questions, the dark pronouncements, the "See you soon." He knew where I lived. He knew my schedule.

Panic seized me. I stumbled around my apartment, frantically locking doors and windows that I hadn't even bothered to latch before. Every creak of the floorboards, every rustle of leaves outside, sent shivers down my spine.

I called the police, my voice trembling as I relayed my story. They assured me they would investigate, but the words felt hollow. I knew I had been a target, and I knew I had escaped, by some miracle, a fate I couldn't bear to contemplate.

The next few weeks were a blur of fear and anxiety. I changed my locks, installed an alarm system, and slept with a baseball bat beside my bed. I avoided going out alone, constantly looking over my shoulder, convinced that he was still out there, watching me.

The fear eventually subsided, replaced by a gnawing sense of unease. How could I have been so blind? How could I have been so easily charmed by a monster? I replayed the date in my mind a thousand times, searching for clues I had missed, for red flags I had ignored.

I never saw Richard Ramirez again. He was eventually captured and brought to justice. But even years later, the memory of that night still haunts me. The candlelight, the dark restaurant, the piercing blue eyes, the chilling promise: "See you soon." A promise I was lucky enough to escape. A promise I would never forget.

"The Butcher of Plainfield"

The Wisconsin air in November 1955 clung to you like a damp shroud, seeping into your bones even through the thickest wool coat. My breath plumed out in front of me as I hauled another bucket of well water back to the house. Life in Plainfield was hard work, but it was honest work. Or so I thought.

We'd only been living next door to Ed Gein for a little over a year. He was a peculiar fellow, kept mostly to himself on that overgrown farm of his. His mother, Augusta, had passed not long before we moved in, and the locals said she'd kept him on a tight leash his whole life. Now, he just seemed…lost. He'd occasionally wave a hand in greeting while I was working in the yard, a shy, almost apologetic gesture. I'd try to return the neighborly courtesy, but there was something about his eyes that made it difficult. They held a disconcerting vacantness, like looking into a well with no bottom.

My wife, Martha, always warned me to keep my distance. "He's not right in the head, Thomas," she'd say, her voice laced with a suspicion I couldn't quite dismiss. She disliked the way he'd stare at her, not lecherously, but with a detached, almost clinical interest.

The farm itself was a testament to his reclusiveness. The house was a dilapidated, two-story affair, paint peeling like sunburnt skin. The yard was a tangled wilderness of weeds and rusted farm equipment, a graveyard for forgotten dreams. I remember thinking, more than once, that it looked like a place where bad things could fester.

The first odd thing I noticed was the silence. You rarely heard livestock on the Gein farm, even though he had a few chickens and a handful of hogs. And the only sound coming from the house was the occasional flicker of the radio at night. Evenings were usually filled with the comforting sounds of family – children laughing, the clatter of dinner preparations, the murmur of conversation. But at the Gein place, it was always unsettlingly quiet.

Then there was the smell. On still days, a faint, sickly-sweet odor would drift over from his property. It was a smell I couldn't quite place, something vaguely organic and decaying. I chalked it up to manure and the general state of neglect on the farm, but it still made my stomach churn.

A few weeks before it all came crashing down, I saw something that truly unnerved me. I was coming home late from a poker game in town, the moon a sliver in the inky sky. As I passed the Gein farm, I saw a light flickering in the barn. Thinking it might be a fire, I pulled over and approached cautiously. I peered through a crack in the barn door, my heart hammering against my ribs.

Inside, Ed was working under the dim glow of a lantern. He was hunched over a workbench, and I could see him meticulously cleaning something. It looked like…a skull.

I froze, a cold dread gripping me. I couldn't be sure, of course, the light was poor, and my mind was playing tricks on me. I backed away slowly, climbed back into my truck, and drove home, my hands shaking. I didn't tell Martha. I was afraid she'd think I was crazy, or worse, that I was somehow involved.

The next day, Bernice Worden, the owner of the hardware store in town, went missing. Ed was one of the last people seen talking to her. The sheriff's men came out to the Gein farm that evening. I remember watching from my porch, a knot of dread tightening in my stomach.

Then the scream. A bloodcurdling, animalistic scream that ripped through the night. It came from the barn.

The sheriff's men poured into the barn, their faces grim. What they found there… well, the papers never told the whole truth. But they told enough. Things that made my skin crawl and my gut churn. Body parts, meticulously crafted into macabre trophies. Chairs upholstered with human skin. Bowls made from skulls. Masks made from faces.

Ed Gein was arrested that night. He confessed to robbing graves, to desecrating corpses. He even admitted to killing Bernice Worden, although his state of mind at the time…well, who could say?

Life in Plainfield changed forever after that. The quiet, isolated town became a place synonymous with horror. We moved away a few months later, unable to bear the weight of the darkness that had settled over the community.

Even now, decades later, I still wake up in a cold sweat, the image of that skull in the barn burned into my memory. I lived next door to Ed Gein. And the silence, the smell, the vacant stare, the bone-chilling secret he kept…it still haunts me. It always will.

"The Green River Killer"

The desk next to mine in Chemistry was always a little…damp. Not soaked, but just a faint, persistent clamminess, like a forgotten gym sock stuffed in a locker. I never said anything. You didn't exactly critique Gary Ridgeway's hygiene. He wasn't someone you wanted to draw attention to.

He was quiet, almost unnervingly so. A low hum seemed to emanate from him rather than actual speech. He wore the same faded blue work shirt and ill-fitting jeans every single day. His eyes were a pale, watery blue, and they seemed to look straight through you.

Back then, in the late 60s, we were all trying to figure things out. Discover our identities, push boundaries, rebel against the expected. Gary seemed immune. He was a void, a blank slate. He never participated in class discussions, never laughed at Mr. Henderson's corny jokes, never expressed an opinion about anything.

He was, in short, forgettable.

Except for the damp desk. And the occasional lingering smell of… pine? That's the best I can describe it. A sharp, almost astringent pine scent that seemed to cling to him.

We were an unlikely pair, bound only by the alphabet. My last name started with a 'Q', his with an 'R'. We were destined for the same row, year after year. I was a bookish, ambitious girl, dreaming of escaping our small town and making my mark. Gary seemed content to simply exist.

One day, during a particularly grueling lab on titration, I fumbled, knocking over a beaker of hydrochloric acid. It splashed onto my hand, burning like fire. I yelped, instinctively pulling back.

21

Before I could even register what was happening, Gary was there. He pulled me to the sink, grabbed the emergency eye wash station (despite it being my hand that was burned), and flushed my hand with cold water for what felt like an eternity.

He didn't say a word. Just held my hand under the stream, his grip surprisingly strong. He seemed utterly focused, his pale blue eyes intense and unwavering. The pine scent seemed stronger then, almost overpowering.

When Mr. Henderson arrived, fussing and clucking, Gary simply stepped back, his face impassive. I stammered my thanks, feeling strangely unnerved by his silent, efficient help.

After that, I tried to be friendly. I'd offer him a stick of gum, or ask him about his weekend. He'd offer a grunt in response, his gaze sliding away. The damp desk remained between us, an invisible barrier.

Then, I left for college. I traded the pines of Washington for the brick and ivy of the East Coast. I thrived, lost myself in studies and new friendships. Gary Ridgeway became a distant memory, a footnote in the story of my youth.

Years later, the name surfaced again, plastered across newspapers and television screens. The Green River Killer. The details were horrifying, the scope unimaginable. The photo they showed… it was him. Older, harder, but undeniably the same Gary Ridgeway who sat next to me in chemistry class.

My stomach churned. The clammy desk, the silent presence, the strange pine scent… they flooded back, amplified by the monstrous reality of what he had become.

I tried to reconcile the quiet, almost invisible boy with the monster who had terrorized our community. I remembered the intense focus in his eyes as he held my hand under the water. Was it genuine concern, or something else, something darker, lurking beneath the surface?

Could I have seen the monster in him then? Could I have, even unconsciously, sensed the darkness that would eventually consume him? The answer, I knew, was no. He had been a cipher, a blank space. A damp desk and a faint pine scent.

But the chilling reality remained. The boy who sat next to me, the boy I barely acknowledged, had been capable of unspeakable evil. And that, more than anything, was what haunted me. He was a reminder of the darkness that can hide in plain sight, even next to you in Advanced Placement Chemistry. And sometimes, the most terrifying monsters are the ones you can't see coming.

"BTK"

The fluorescent hum of the Wichita Public Library was usually a comforting drone, a soundtrack to the rustling of pages and the quiet click of keyboards. That day, though, it felt oppressive, like a judgemental buzz aimed directly at my skull. I was researching local hauntings, specifically the legend of the "Shadow Man" said to stalk the abandoned grain elevators near the river. A niche interest, I knew, but one that fueled my love for a good scare and a decent story.

I was hunched over a microfilm reader, squinting at blurry newspaper articles from the 70s, when I felt a presence beside me. I straightened, expecting a librarian wanting to tell me I was hogging the machine again. Instead, I saw him.

He was an older man, maybe late 60s, with a neatly trimmed mustache and kind eyes that crinkled at the corners. He wore a beige cardigan over a button-down shirt and khaki pants. Nothing remarkable. He looked…ordinary. The kind of man you'd see tending his garden or volunteering at the church.

"Excuse me," he said, his voice a low, almost hesitant rumble. "I couldn't help but notice you were reading about local history. Are you interested in the BTK case?"

My blood ran cold. The BTK case. Even now, over thirty years after the reign of terror, the letters were heavy, laden with fear and a collective grief that hung over Wichita like a perpetual storm cloud. I hadn't mentioned the letters at all.

"No, not exactly," I mumbled, trying to appear nonchalant. "Just looking into the history of the grain elevators."

He chuckled, a dry, rustling sound. "Oh, those old things. They've seen a lot, haven't they? Wichita's seen a lot. Myself included." He paused, his gaze drifting towards a window that overlooked the parking lot. "I used to work for the city, you know. Animal Control. Saw a lot of…strays."

The way he lingered on the word "strays" sent a shiver down my spine. He wasn't making direct threats, but the implication was undeniable. It felt like he was testing the waters, gauging my reaction.

"That's…interesting," I managed. Every instinct screamed at me to leave, to bolt out of the library and never look back. But something else, a morbid curiosity, held me rooted to the spot.

He extended his hand. "Dennis," he said. "Dennis Rader."

My breath caught in my throat. Dennis Rader. The name echoed in my mind, a litany of horrors. BTK. Bind, Torture, Kill. The man who had taunted the police with his cryptic messages, the man who had terrorized Wichita for decades, was standing right next to me, offering his hand.

I hesitated for a fraction of a second, then shook his hand, the action feeling surreal. His grip was surprisingly firm, calloused.

"Nice to meet you," I croaked, my voice barely a whisper.

He smiled, a disturbingly benign expression. "So, the grain elevators, huh? They're full of stories. Dark stories, most likely." He leaned closer, his voice dropping to a conspiratorial whisper. "Sometimes, the darkest stories are the most interesting, don't you think?"

He continued to talk, rambling about the history of Wichita, the changing landscape, the good old days. He sprinkled his monologue with chillingly offhand remarks about control, power, and the darkness that lurks beneath the surface of everyday life. He talked about how important documentation was, how easily things could be forgotten if they weren't properly recorded. It was a carefully crafted performance, designed to unsettle, to intimidate.

All the while, I was mentally screaming, desperately trying to formulate a plan. I couldn't just run. He might follow. I needed to be calm, to think.

Finally, after what felt like an eternity, he seemed to tire. "Well," he said, patting my arm with a disturbingly familiar gesture, "it was nice talking to you. I should be going."

He turned to leave, then paused, looking back at me with those unsettlingly kind eyes. "Remember," he said, "some stories are best left untold."

He walked away, disappearing into the anonymous rows of bookshelves. I stood there, frozen, my heart hammering against my ribs.

I didn't go back to the microfilm reader. I didn't continue my research on the Shadow Man. Instead, I went to the nearest police station and told them everything. They listened intently, taking copious notes. They knew him, of course. He was a fixture in the community, a seemingly harmless old man.

Afterwards, I felt a little safer, but the encounter left a permanent scar. The fluorescent hum of the library would never sound quite the same again. I'd learned that day that monsters don't always wear masks and wield knives. Sometimes, they wear cardigans and offer you a friendly handshake in the middle of the library. And sometimes, the most terrifying thing is not what they do, but what they imply. The chilling suggestion that darkness can hide in plain sight, waiting for the right moment to reveal itself. The knowledge that evil can be incredibly, disturbingly...ordinary.

"LEE"

The vinyl stuck to my thighs, a clammy embrace on that sweltering Florida afternoon. August humidity hung thick, a visible miasma clinging to everything, even the inside of the Greyhound bus. I was nineteen, running away from a small-town life I felt was suffocating me, chasing a dream of... something. Anything, really.

She sat across the aisle, three rows ahead. I noticed her immediately. Maybe it was the way she sat, hunched and wary, like a stray dog expecting to be kicked. Or maybe it was the hardness in her eyes, a glint that belied the faded denim jacket and the desperate grip she held on a crumpled paper bag.

She chain-smoked Marlboro Reds, the acrid smell mingling with the artificial lemon scent of the bus's air freshener. With each drag, her face seemed to etch itself a little deeper into the lines of hard living. I caught her staring at me a couple of times. Long, intense stares that made me want to shrink into my seat.

The bus rumbled onward, devouring miles of cracked asphalt. The Florida landscape blurred past in a monotonous green and brown. Somewhere around Ocala, she got up and walked to the back, presumably to use the bathroom. When she returned, she stopped at my seat.

"Got a light?" she rasped, her voice surprisingly low and gravelly.

I rummaged in my backpack and produced my zippo. She leaned in close, the scent of cheap perfume and stale cigarettes filling my nostrils. The flame flickered, illuminating her face for a fleeting moment. I saw the raw, untamed desperation there, the palpable hunger that had nothing to do with food.

"Thanks," she said, her eyes holding mine for a beat too long. "Name's Lee."

"Sandra," I replied, then instantly regretted revealing anything.

She nodded, and something like a smile flickered across her lips before vanishing. She went back to her seat, and I tried to lose myself in my Walkman, Bruce Springsteen blasting in my ears.

We didn't talk much after that. Just a few occasional glances across the aisle. I saw her buy a watery coffee and a stale donut at a rest stop. I watched her argue with the bus driver about the volume of his radio. I noticed the way she wrapped her arms around herself when the air conditioning blasted too cold.

As the sun began to set, painting the sky in bruised purples and oranges, the bus pulled into a small, desolate town. Bunnell, I think it was. Lee got off. She didn't look back. She just stepped onto the dusty pavement and disappeared into the gathering darkness.

I rode on, my heart pounding in my chest. I felt a strange mix of relief and unease. Something about her had unnerved me, had left me with a lingering feeling of dread.

Years later, I was flipping through channels when I saw her face on the news. They were talking about a series of murders, highway robberies, and a woman named Aileen Wuornos. The face was older, harder, but undeniably the same woman who had asked me for a light on that Greyhound bus.

My blood ran cold. "Lee," she had said. It was an alias, a flimsy shield against the life she was living.

I replayed that bus ride in my head a thousand times. I wondered what had been going through her mind that day. Had she already committed her first murder? Was I in any danger?

The vinyl of the bus seat, the smell of Marlboro Reds, the hardness in her eyes – those details remained etched in my memory. I'd shared a brief, insignificant moment with a monster. And that knowledge, more than anything else, changed the course of my own life. It reminded me that even in the most mundane circumstances, darkness can lurk just around the corner, waiting for a flicker of light. And sometimes, the most dangerous thing you can do is offer it.

The Axman of New Orleans

I was seventeen the first time I saw him.

It was late summer in New Orleans, the kind of night where the air feels thick enough to swallow, and even the streetlights look like they're struggling to stay awake. I'd snuck out of the little shotgun house I shared with my mom and nana, heart racing with rebellion and the thrill of wandering the Quarter alone. I didn't have a destination—just a need to be somewhere that didn't smell like fried okra and mothballs.

That's when I heard the music.

Not jazz, like you'd expect in New Orleans, but something older, slower…like a lullaby hummed through a cracked phonograph. It echoed from an alley between two weathered buildings. And like something out of a bad idea, I followed it.

He was standing at the end of the alley. A tall man, frame hidden beneath a long black coat, hat pulled low. I couldn't see his face, but I felt his eyes—sharp and heavy like hooks in my skin. There was something in his hand. A case, maybe. Or a sack. I told myself it was a musician's bag. Maybe he was just another street performer with a flair for theatrics. But deep down, I knew.

He stepped forward, slow and deliberate, and the music stopped like it had hit a wall. The air shifted. Colder. The sounds of Bourbon Street seemed to vanish behind me. All I could hear was my own heartbeat and the faint creak of his shoes against the cobblestone.

I turned and ran.

My shoes slapped against the street, my lungs burning. I didn't stop until I hit Esplanade, where the lights were a little brighter and the laughter a little louder. I looked back. No one followed. But I swear I could still feel him, lingering, like the scent of smoke after a fire.

Years later, I saw a sketch in an old book about unsolved crimes in Louisiana. The hat, the coat, the eyes I never saw but somehow still remember.

The Axman of New Orleans.

Maybe it wasn't him. Maybe I was just a dumb kid chasing shadows and stories. But deep down, I believe it. I believe I met something evil that night. Something ancient. Something that waits in the cracks of the world, behind closed doors, hoping someone foolish enough will come knocking.

That night, it almost had me.

The Butcher Baker

I didn't know who he was until years later. Back then, I just thought he was a weird little man with bad manners and kind eyes that didn't quite match his smile.

I was working the counter at a diner in Anchorage the summer I turned nineteen. I'd taken the job on a whim, wanting something different, something colder and quieter than the heat and noise I'd grown up in. The tourists came and went, truckers and hunters too, but there were regulars—mostly older men with hands like rawhide and stories soaked in whiskey.

He was one of them.

Came in around the same time every week, always ordered the same thing: black coffee, two eggs over easy, and sourdough toast. He never ate the toast. He'd just sit there, picking at the crusts, scribbling in a little leather notebook with a pen that looked older than I was.

He told me his name was Bob. Just Bob. He liked to talk—about flying, mostly. How the world looked different from the air. "Peaceful," he'd say. "You'd be surprised how small everything seems when you're looking down on it." I thought he was just a bush pilot. That kind of guy was common in Alaska. Normal. Harmless.

Until the day he asked if I wanted to go flying with him.

Something about the way he said it made my skin crawl. My stomach twisted up. He smiled, but there was a tightness behind it, like his face wasn't used to moving that way. My heart pounded, and I laughed it off, said I was scared of heights. He said, "Well, maybe some girls aren't meant to fly." And just like that, he slid a twenty under his untouched toast and walked out.

I never saw him again.

Years later, I was flipping through a true crime book at a friend's house, and there he was. Robert Hansen. The Butcher Baker. The pilot who'd hunt women in the Alaskan wilderness like prey. I dropped the book. My mouth went dry.

I didn't tell anyone for a long time. Who'd believe me? That he sat across from me sipping coffee while thinking about murder. That I served a killer eggs and toast and smiled while doing it. That I got lucky.

That I didn't say yes.

Sometimes I wonder how many girls didn't feel that twist in their gut. How many said yes because he seemed...normal. Quiet. Kind of sweet.

Sometimes monsters don't look like monsters. They just look like Bob.

The Angel of Death

I was twenty-one when I met Dr. Shipman. Just out of college, living in Manchester for the summer with a friend, trying to figure out what came next. I came down with the flu—or at least, I thought it was the flu. Fever, dizziness, aches in every inch of my body. I finally caved and went to the clinic, and they sent me straight to the hospital.

That's where I met him.

He introduced himself simply: "Dr. Shipman." No first name, no smile. His eyes were flat, unreadable, but he spoke with a calm authority that made you sit up and listen. He took my pulse, listened to my chest, scribbled something in a file, and told the nurse to admit me overnight. I remember thinking he had the kind of voice that made you feel like everything would be okay.

And that's what he did—he made me feel okay.

He came to check on me twice during that stay. Both times, his presence filled the room like heavy fog. Quiet, but suffocating. He didn't ask many questions. Just observed. Like he was trying to figure me out.

Once, he touched my wrist gently after taking my blood pressure and said, "You'll be just fine." I didn't think much of it then. I was young, naive, and sick. What else would a doctor say?

I was discharged the next morning. No fanfare. I didn't even get to say goodbye. Just a different doctor bringing my papers, telling me to rest and drink fluids. I went back to my apartment and never thought about him again.

Not until a few years later when his face was all over the news.

Harold Shipman. The quiet, respected doctor who had killed over 200 patients. I sat on the floor of my living room, the remote slipping from my hand, as the news anchor listed names and towns. He hadn't just treated people—he'd chosen them. Decided when they'd die. And done it with a syringe and a soft voice.

My stomach turned. I couldn't breathe. My brain kept circling the same question: Why didn't he choose me?

Was I too young? Too healthy? Did something about me make him pause?

I'll never know.

But I carry that brush with death like a scar no one can see. I didn't escape a monster in the woods. I didn't run screaming down a dark alley. I just got lucky. I met a killer—and he let me go.

Sometimes I think about the other patients. The ones who weren't so lucky. The ones who trusted him completely. And I wonder how different my story could've been—if he'd decided I wouldn't be "just fine."

The Grim Sleeper

I should've trusted my gut. That's what I keep telling myself when I think about that night. I was nineteen, broke, and crashing on a friend's couch in South Los Angeles. It was the kind of summer heat that stuck to your skin and made everything feel slower... heavier. I had just gotten off a late shift at the diner, and my friend hadn't shown up to walk me home like she promised. My phone was dead. Typical.

So I walked.

The streets were quiet. Not the good kind of quiet—eerily quiet. Like the city was holding its breath. That's when I noticed the car. Old, boxy, dark. Creeping slow behind me like it had nowhere better to be.

I crossed the street.

So did he.

I started walking faster, my heart pounding in my ears. And then, just as I reached the mouth of an alley, the car cut in front of me and stopped. The door opened.

I froze.

He didn't look like a monster. He looked like someone's uncle. Calm. Older. Wearing work clothes and a hat pulled low. He smiled—like he knew me. Like I was expected.

"You okay? Need a ride?" he asked.

His voice was soft. Too soft. The kind of voice that disarmed you before you even realized you should run.

"No, I'm good," I said, stepping back.

"You sure? Not safe for girls to be out here alone at night."

That was rich—coming from the man literally making it unsafe.

I remember every detail about his eyes. Cold. Dead. Not angry, not desperate—just *empty*. I knew, in that moment, if I got in that car, no one would ever see me again.

So I lied. I told him someone was coming for me. That my dad was a cop. That my friend's house had a camera pointed right at the street. I threw every desperate bluff I could think of.

And for whatever reason… he just stared at me for a few seconds. Then he laughed—low and hollow—and drove away like nothing happened.

I collapsed onto the curb and cried for a long time.

Years later, when they finally caught him—**Lonnie David Franklin Jr.**—I saw the photo and almost threw up. It was him. The man in the car. The Grim Sleeper. A serial killer who stalked the streets for *decades*, picking off women who looked just like me.

I was one blink, one breath, one bad decision away from being one of his forgotten victims.

But I lived.

And I'll never forget the way evil looked me right in the face—and smiled.

The Terminator

Back in the winter of 1996, I was driving my old Volga as a private cab around Zhytomyr. Nothing official—just enough to put bread on the table for my wife and our baby girl. Those were hard times. The Soviet Union had fallen, and everything felt... unmoored. Factories had shut down, crime was rising, and people were desperate. Men like me took whatever jobs we could find. And sometimes, we picked up the wrong passengers.

It was a Tuesday night, just after eleven. Snow dusted the roads like powdered chalk, and the whole city was wrapped in that quiet that only comes in deep winter. I had just dropped off a fare near a small village on the outskirts when I saw a man walking along the road, thumb out. No car in sight for miles. I thought maybe he was heading home from the train station or trying to make it to the next town. He looked harmless—mid-thirties, average build, wearing a long coat and a cap pulled low.

I pulled over. "Where to?" I asked.

He said the name of a village I didn't recognize, somewhere near Lviv. I told him I could take him part of the way. He nodded and got in.

The first few minutes were quiet. Too quiet. He didn't ask me anything, didn't make small talk. Just sat there, staring out the window like he was memorizing the landscape. I offered him a cigarette to break the silence, but he declined. Said he didn't smoke. Said it "dulled the senses."

His Ukrainian was clean, educated—but something about the way he spoke... it made my skin crawl.

Then he asked me if I believed in fate.

I laughed it off, said something about how fate hadn't done much for the working man lately. He looked at me and said,

"Sometimes fate chooses who lives and who dies. Sometimes, I'm just the one who makes it happen faster."

That's when my stomach turned.

I knew there'd been killings. Whole families murdered in their homes, even children. The news called it the work of a madman, someone moving from village to village leaving no one alive. They said he used a shotgun. That he didn't just kill—he *exterminated*. And they gave him a name:

"The Terminator."

That was the moment I knew. It was him. **Anatoly Onoprienko.**

My hands gripped the wheel so tight my knuckles went white. Every instinct screamed at me to throw him out of the car. But I stayed calm. Acted like I hadn't caught the reference. Like I didn't recognize his face from the sketches in the papers. I played dumb. Prayed harder than I ever had in my life.

When we reached the crossroads, I told him I couldn't go farther. Blamed a fake fuel gauge issue. He stared at me for a second that felt like an hour, then quietly opened the door and stepped out. No thank you. No goodbye.

He just disappeared into the snow-covered trees.

Two weeks later, they caught him. I remember sitting at the kitchen table with my wife, watching the news in stunned silence. Same coat. Same face. Same cold eyes.

I never told her I gave *The Terminator* a ride that night. What would've been the point? He was a monster disguised as a man… and I was just a cab driver who got lucky.

But some nights, when the snow falls just right and the road's too quiet, I still see his silhouette walking along the shoulder—and I keep on driving.

The Red Ripper

It was the fall of 1989 when I had my brush with a monster. I was twenty years old, living in Rostov-on-Don, doing odd jobs to get by. Nothing steady—whatever paid enough for bread, vodka, and rent. That evening, I was coming back from a long day hauling crates at the rail yard. The air was sharp, the sun low, and the streets near the station were practically empty. That was typical. People didn't linger back then. Not with all the talk going around.

You see, folks had been whispering about the murders—bodies found near train stations, in the woods, in ditches. Most of them were kids, women. Nobody ever saw anything. Just death. They called him a ghost. A phantom. The press was careful not to stir up panic, but we all knew. Someone was hunting.

I just didn't know that I'd come face-to-face with him.

I was walking past the edge of the train yard when I saw this man standing alone by the benches. Tallish, glasses, drab coat. Nothing unusual. He looked like someone's uncle, honestly—quiet, awkward. He caught my eye and asked if I knew when the next train to Shakhty was. I told him it had already gone. Then he asked if I could help him carry something—said he dropped his bag by the woods trying to avoid a group of drunks.

Normally, I'd have kept walking. But something about him... he didn't seem threatening. Just off. So I said sure.

We crossed the tracks and walked toward the trees. That's when the hairs on my neck started to rise. He asked if I lived nearby, if I had family. He smiled, but it didn't reach his eyes. Then he stopped walking, looked down at the leaves, and said something I'll never forget.

"You seem smart. I usually choose the foolish ones."

I froze.

My legs felt like stone. My mouth went dry. I didn't know what to do, what to say. I forced out a nervous laugh, said something like, "You joking, man?" But I could see it in his eyes. He wasn't joking.

I don't know why he let me go. Maybe because I didn't run. Maybe because I didn't challenge him. I told him I needed to get back before my boss noticed I was late. I turned and walked away, fast but calm. I didn't hear him follow.

He vanished into the trees.

It wasn't until a year later that I saw his face again—on the news. **Andrei Chikatilo.** The Butcher of Rostov. The *Red Ripper*. Responsible for more than fifty deaths. And there he was, that same drab coat, that same face, staring out from the screen like a bad dream brought to life.

Sometimes I think he wanted me to know. To see him. To *almost* be one of his stories. But I walked away. I got lucky.

And now, I never walk near train yards after dark. Not even thirty years later.

The Crossbow Cannibal

It was raining the night I met Stephen Griffiths. Not the kind of soft, romantic drizzle you see in movies—this was a cold, slapping rain that felt like it was trying to scrub you off the face of the earth. I was working security at a quiet student housing complex in Bradford, England. It wasn't much—just checking cameras, making rounds, the usual routine. Boring, mostly. But boredom was a blessing, and I didn't realize how much I cherished it until that night.

He came in around 2 a.m. Long black coat, hood up, soaking wet. I remember thinking he looked like a man who wanted to disappear into the shadows. He told me he was visiting a student and gave a name. I checked the registry. No one by that name lived there. He smiled, almost like he expected that. Said maybe he had the wrong building, and turned to leave.

But I felt something. Not fear, exactly—more like instinct flaring in the back of my mind. There was something off about him. He didn't seem surprised. He wasn't drunk, wasn't confused. He was calm. Too calm. I watched him on the cameras after he left. He didn't go to the next building or check a phone. He just walked down the alley and disappeared.

A few days later, the news broke. They found body parts in the River Aire. Three women. Missing for months. Pieces had been showing up one at a time—bits of bone, flesh, sometimes just a shoe—but now they had a suspect. A name.

Stephen Griffiths.

Also known as **The Crossbow Cannibal**.

I stared at the mugshot on the screen and my blood turned cold. That was him. The man who stood right in front of me, dripping rain on the front desk, looking like nothing more than another face passing through.

They said he filmed one of the killings. Said he posed as a researcher in criminology, studying serial killers. Said he was fascinated with Peter Sutcliffe and others like him. But he wasn't just fascinated. He was trying to become one of them.

And he almost slipped right past me.

Sometimes I wonder what would've happened if I hadn't checked the registry, if I'd just buzzed him in. Would he have added another victim that night? Would my face be among the missing?

I never saw him again. But I still dream of him sometimes—of that moment, that look, that smile. Like he knew something I didn't.

Like he'd already made up his mind.

The Cromwell Street Killers

I worked construction one summer in Gloucester. Nothing fancy — mostly hauling bricks, cleaning up sites. The crew used to take breaks on the curb outside this old, beat-up house on Cromwell Street. Number 25. Back then, I had no idea what had gone on inside.

It was always quiet there. Curtains drawn. Garden overgrown. Once, I saw a girl, maybe fifteen, peeking out from the second-story window. She didn't wave or smile. Just looked at us like we were ghosts. One of the guys on the crew said the people who lived there were weird. "Rose and Fred," he said. "Keeps to themselves."

A few years later, I saw it all unravel on TV. *"The House of Horrors."* That's what they called it. Bodies beneath the floorboards. Torture. Abuse. I couldn't believe it — I had sat on their sidewalk, drank soda twenty feet from hell, and never knew.

Rosemary West and her husband, Fred, were monsters hiding in plain sight. They didn't look like killers. They looked like anyone's neighbors. And that was the scariest part.

Sometimes, when I think back to that girl in the window, I wonder if she was already gone. If I saw a ghost that day. Or worse — someone who knew no one was coming to help her.

The Purple Satin Killer

I was working late at the diner off Route 22, the kind of place where the coffee's always lukewarm, and the jukebox hasn't worked in years. It was a slow night until he walked in—tall, with a calm demeanor that didn't quite match the storm in his eyes. He slid into a booth, ordered black coffee, and sat there, staring out the window as if waiting for something—or someone.

We made small talk. He said his name was Jonas, just passing through. There was something about him, a quiet intensity that made the hairs on my neck stand up. When he left, I noticed a torn piece of purple satin on the seat. I thought it was odd but didn't think much of it.

A week later, the news broke about the "Purple Satin Killer." Twenty-three women across five states, all found with a piece of purple satin. The composite sketch flashed on the screen—it was him. Jonas Williker.

I still think about that night. How close I was to evil, how a simple piece of fabric could hold so much terror. Behind closed doors, monsters wear human faces.

The Golden State Killer

I was twelve when my mom made us move into that little house outside Citrus Heights. Said we needed a fresh start. She never really told me why, but I figured it out later — my dad was afraid. Not of anyone in particular, just of what people were becoming. What they were capable of.

We didn't have much, but the neighborhood was quiet, almost too quiet. One night, I woke up to the sound of someone walking around outside. I thought it was a raccoon, maybe a neighbor's cat. But then I saw the handle of our back sliding door jiggle. Slowly. Like someone was testing it. I froze. Didn't breathe. I couldn't see a face, just a silhouette. Tall. Still. Watching.

My mom called the police the next day, but there was nothing to report. Nothing taken. No prints. Just that feeling. That awful, crawling feeling like someone had been too close.

Years later, the world found out what had been living in the dark. Joseph James DeAngelo — the Golden State Killer. Former cop. Husband. Father. Monster. They say he broke into homes, tied up husbands, raped wives, killed without blinking. Sometimes he stole little things — a button, a photo, a single earring. Just enough to make you wonder if you'd imagined it.

When his name hit the news, something in my mom broke. She didn't say much, but I saw it in her eyes. That same fear my dad carried. The kind that doesn't go away — not even after they catch him.

I still keep a chair wedged under my bedroom door, even though I live across the country now. I still double-check the windows. Because once you know someone like Joseph DeAngelo existed — someone who watched you while you slept — you never really feel safe again.

The 60 Freeway Killer

It was the fall of '93 when I made the worst mistake of my life.

I was working the closing shift at a diner off Valley Boulevard in Industry. Didn't have a car, so I walked to the bus stop at the edge of the 60 Freeway. It was late, and I was tired — too tired to notice the dark blue sedan parked across the street with the engine idling.

He pulled up just as I was checking the bus schedule. Rolled down the window and said, "You need a ride? Not safe out here this late."

I hesitated. His voice was calm, friendly even. He looked like somebody's uncle. Clean shirt, short haircut. Said his name was Ray. I should've said no. But I got in.

We didn't head toward my neighborhood. Instead, he took the on-ramp to the freeway, his hands steady on the wheel, eyes fixed ahead. I asked him where he was going — he smiled like I was joking. That smile... I still see it sometimes when I close my eyes.

"You ever see the city from the overlook?" he asked.

I said I didn't want to go. I told him I was tired. That I had people waiting. That I didn't feel right.

He didn't answer. Just kept driving. I started watching the exit signs, memorizing every one. At the next light, I told him I was going to be sick. I begged him to let me out. He didn't say anything. Didn't even look at me.

I don't know what gave him pause — maybe he sensed I was going to jump from the car, maybe he didn't want a scene. But he pulled off near Diamond Bar and told me to "walk it off." I slammed the door and ran. Didn't look back once. A trucker at a gas station let me use his phone, and I called my sister.

For years, I told people I was just lucky — got picked up by a weirdo, nothing more. But in 2007, a detective came to my door. Said they'd identified a man responsible for multiple murders of women, all dumped along the 60 Freeway from the late '80s through the '90s. Said his name was **Ivan Hill**.

The name meant nothing to me, but when he showed me a photo… I nearly dropped the glass in my hand. That face, that smile — it was *him*. "Ray."

He'd killed at least six women. Maybe more. I wasn't supposed to walk away from that car. I wasn't supposed to grow up, get married, or tell this story.

But I did.

And now, every time I see the 60 Freeway in the rearview, I don't think of traffic or the smoggy skyline. I think of how close I came to becoming a headline — and how monsters like Ivan Hill look just like the man who offers you a ride home.

49

The Acid Bath Murderer

My gran used to tell me not to trust men in good suits. Said the real monsters don't growl — they charm you. Smile while they unlock the cellar door.

In 1948, she was working at a dress shop in Hammersmith. Said it paid well enough for tea, rent, and a few nice things. One evening, a man came in just before closing — tall, polished, handsome in a sharp three-piece suit. He complimented the window display and asked if they offered tailoring services. She told him no, but he kept chatting, warm and well-spoken, like someone born into money. His name, he said, was Mr. Haigh.

Over the next few weeks, he stopped in often. Always bought something small — a tie, cufflinks, once even a ladies' silk scarf "for his mother." He asked about her family, her dreams, and eventually if she'd ever considered making more money. Said he had a business opportunity, a position assisting him with property clients who were "inconveniently rich and frequently abroad."

She told me she almost went with him once. He'd offered to pick her up at the shop and take her to see the office in Crawley. Said he had paperwork, something to sign. But the morning he was supposed to come, her youngest brother took ill, and she had to stay home. She said it was the first and only time she ever felt thankful for sickness.

Weeks later, police came to the shop asking about a man named John George Haigh.

He'd murdered six — maybe nine — people. Dissolved their bodies in sulfuric acid, kept their possessions, and forged documents to steal their estates. All that was left of his victims were a few body parts. Teeth. Gallstones. Things acid couldn't eat.

Gran didn't cry when she told me. She just smoked and looked out the window like she was trying to see back in time. Said, *"He looked at me like he already owned my bones."*

They caught him eventually, locked him up for good. But sometimes I wonder if Gran ever went through her things and found something he gave her — a scarf, a ring, something that once belonged to someone else. Someone he melted down to silence.

She never married. Said men were too slippery to hold onto. But every year, on the anniversary of his arrest, she lit a candle in the kitchen window and left it burning all night.

Not for him.

For the ones who never got to tell their story.

The Boxcar Killer

I met him in a rail yard outside Eugene, Oregon, during a winter that bit straight through your boots. We were part of the same invisible crowd — the forgotten, the ones who lived between towns and train schedules. I was just eighteen, running from something I didn't have the guts to face back home. He said his name was "RJ," and he looked like someone who'd been on the move a long time.

RJ shared his fire and a can of Dinty Moore stew he'd stolen from a gas station. He talked soft, like every word had to sneak past something darker inside him. We rode together a few days, swapping stories, watching out for bulls, sleeping under stars that felt too far away to matter.

There was something off about him, though. He never really slept. Just sat up, carving shapes into wood with a switchblade that never left his hand. He'd ask weird questions, too — about people I'd met, who I trusted, where I kept my things. At the time, I thought he was just cautious. We all were.

One night, in a yard outside Redding, I woke up to find him gone. So was my backpack. So was Danny — a kid who'd been with us since Portland. I found his body three days later, face down in a ditch behind the grain elevator. His throat was cut, and his boots were missing.

I didn't stick around after that.

Years later, I saw his face on the news. They were calling him **Robert Joseph Silveria Jr.** — *The Boxcar Killer.* Said he killed more than a dozen transients, maybe more, across California, Oregon, Utah, Wyoming... wherever the rails could take him. All fellow drifters. All people no one would miss until someone found the smell.

The cops said he had a thing about "cleansing the rails." Like some kind of twisted prophet. But I knew better. RJ wasn't trying to save anyone. He was just a wolf who'd figured out that the best place to hunt is where no one's looking.

I kept moving after that. Never stayed in one place long. Still don't. You learn fast out here — the ones with the quiet eyes, the ones who share their fire too easily — they're the ones to keep your distance from.

Because out here, ghosts don't haunt you.

Men like Silveria do.

The Candyman

I was seventeen when I first heard about the man they called the Candyman. It was the summer of 1973, and Houston was sweltering under a relentless sun. I had just moved into a modest apartment complex in the Heights, eager to start my first job at a local hardware store.

The neighborhood was a mix of old charm and quiet decay. Children played in the streets, and neighbors exchanged pleasantries over fences. It felt safe, almost idyllic.

One evening, after a long shift, I stopped by a small convenience store to grab a cold drink. As I approached the counter, the clerk, a middle-aged man with a weary smile, handed me a piece of candy.

"On the house," he said.

I hesitated, but he insisted. "Just a little something sweet to end your day."

I took the candy, thanked him, and left.

Over the next few weeks, I noticed subtle changes. Strangers lingered near the store, watching. I received anonymous notes slipped under my door—simple messages like "Enjoy the sweets?" and "More to come."

Unease settled in. I started taking different routes home, avoiding the store, and keeping to myself.

Then, one night, I heard a knock at my door. I peered through the peephole to see a man in his thirties, neatly dressed, holding a small box.

"Sorry to bother you," he said. "I believe this was delivered to me by mistake."

He handed me the box and left.

Inside was an assortment of candies, each wrapped meticulously. No note, no explanation.

The next morning, news broke of a man named Dean Corll, dubbed the Candyman, who had been killed by one of his accomplices. Details emerged of his heinous crimes, and the neighborhood buzzed with shock and disbelief.

I never opened the box. I took it to the police, who assured me they'd investigate. But I never heard back.

To this day, I wonder how close I came to becoming one of his victims. The memory of that summer lingers, a chilling reminder that evil often wears a friendly face.

The Candlelight Killer

I was a psychiatric nurse at Metropolitan State Hospital in Norwalk, California, during the late 1960s. The facility housed a mix of patients, some battling inner demons, others placed there by the court system. Among them was a young man named Robert Liberty.

Robert was quiet, almost too quiet. He had a disarming smile and a penchant for sketching intricate candle designs in his notebook. He rarely spoke, but when he did, it was with a calmness that belied the turmoil beneath.

One evening, during my rounds, I found a drawing slipped under my office door. It depicted a room bathed in candlelight, with a figure lying serenely on a couch, surrounded by flickering flames. The detail was hauntingly precise.

I confronted Robert about the drawing. He looked up, eyes distant, and said, "It's a memory."

I reported the incident, but it was dismissed as artistic expression. After all, many patients used art as therapy.

In 1969, Robert was deemed rehabilitated and released. I thought little of it until news broke of a series of murders in Southern California. The victims were found in settings eerily similar to Robert's drawing—posed, surrounded by candles, with messages scrawled nearby.

The media dubbed the perpetrator the "Candlelight Killer."

I couldn't shake the feeling that Robert was involved. I reached out to the authorities, sharing my experiences and the drawing. They listened but had little to go on.

Months later, Robert was apprehended in Colorado after a botched robbery. He was linked to the murders and brought back to California to await trial.

I was called to testify, recounting my interactions with him. It was surreal, seeing him in the courtroom, the same disarming smile on his face.

Before the trial concluded, Robert was killed by a fellow inmate. The details were murky, but some said it was vigilante justice.

Years have passed, but I still keep that drawing. It's a reminder of the darkness that can hide behind the most unassuming faces and the importance of trusting one's instincts.

The Cross Country Killer

It was the fall of 1987 when I first met the Rogers brothers. I had just turned 20 and was working a dead-end job at a small gas station just off Route 7, about 40 miles outside of Cincinnati. It was the kind of job you take when you're trying to figure out life. Long shifts, late nights, and an endless stream of strangers passing through — people who never stuck around long enough to make you feel comfortable.

That night, it was chilly, the kind of cold that sneaks up on you before you realize it. The station was nearly empty, save for a trucker who'd been parked outside for hours. I didn't think much of it. My life back then was full of boring details, and the usual weirdness of late-night gas stations didn't phase me. But when the brothers walked in, something about them just didn't sit right.

Glen was tall, with an intense look in his eyes — like someone who'd seen more than they should have and wasn't about to forget it. His brother Clay was the opposite, shorter, quieter, but there was something unsettling about him too — like he was always watching you from the corner of his eye.

They came in just before closing time. Glen was the first to speak.

"Can we get a couple of sandwiches?" he asked, his voice low and calm. I nodded and walked behind the counter to get the food, trying to keep the feeling that something was off in check. But as I made the sandwiches, Glen stayed close, leaning against the counter, and started talking about the road.

He said he and Clay were just passing through, looking for work in the area. But there was something in the way he spoke that made me uncomfortable. He kept glancing over at Clay as if there was some unspoken understanding between them, like I wasn't supposed to know what they were really about.

"Got any good places around here to stop?" Glen asked, almost like a challenge, as if testing me. I was just a kid, working late at a dead-end job, and here was this guy, staring at me like he knew things I didn't, like he had a secret.

"Not much here," I said, trying to keep it casual. "A few motels down the road. That's about it."

Clay nodded, though he hadn't spoken a word. He just stood there, a little too still for comfort. When I handed over their sandwiches, I noticed the faintest smile on Glen's lips. It wasn't the smile of someone who was just passing through. It was like he knew something I didn't — something dark. Something... final.

As they left, I noticed Glen's eyes linger on me for a moment longer than necessary. That feeling crept back again, that sense of being seen, but not in a way that made me feel safe. I didn't know it then, but I'd just met the man who would eventually be known as the "Cross Country Killer."

I didn't think about it much at the time, just another strange encounter on the job, another two drifters who'd come and gone. It wasn't until years later, when the news broke about Glen Rogers — and the horrifying crimes he'd committed — that I realized the full weight of that brief meeting.

By the time I found out what he had done, I could barely sleep at night without remembering how strange that conversation had been. Glen Rogers, the man who was quietly plotting his future as a killer, had stood there, right in front of me, and I had no idea. He was just another drifter, asking about the area, making small talk — and all the while, something in his eyes told me he was already planning the next step in his dark journey.

The worst part? It wasn't just the fact that I met him. It was that I'd also met Clay — the brother who later testified against him, but who seemed so much a part of the madness that I still can't shake the feeling that both of them were already something beyond human that night. Even now, when I think back to that night, I can't help but feel a shiver.

Because when I look at the news reports and hear about the bodies found across the country, I realize something: I was never meant to walk into that gas station. I was never meant to meet them. But somehow, I did. And I'm still haunted by the idea that for a moment, I was one of the few who unknowingly crossed paths with a killer on his way to becoming something much worse.

The Photographer

It was a late summer evening in 1978 when I first met him. I was a 22-year-old college student, working part-time at a small bookstore in downtown Los Angeles. The store was quiet that night, the kind of evening where time seems to stretch and the air feels thick with anticipation.

He walked in just before closing, his presence immediately noticeable. Tall, with dark, wavy hair and a confident stride, he exuded an unsettling charm. He introduced himself as "John," a photographer looking to expand his portfolio. His eyes, sharp and calculating, seemed to assess everything and everyone in the room.

We exchanged pleasantries, and he mentioned he was looking for models for a new project. He spoke with such authority, his words smooth and persuasive, that I found myself intrigued despite a nagging feeling that something was off. He showed me a leather-bound portfolio filled with photographs—beautiful, haunting images of women in various poses. The artistry was undeniable, but there was an intensity to the photographs that unsettled me.

He suggested we meet the following afternoon to discuss the project further. I agreed, still unsure why I felt both drawn to and repelled by him.

The next day, I met him at a small café near the bookstore. He was already there, sitting at a corner table, his eyes scanning the room. We talked for hours about photography, art, and life. He was engaging, his conversation captivating, but there was an underlying tension in his demeanor. He seemed to study me, his gaze lingering a moment too long, his questions probing deeper than necessary.

As the meeting ended, he handed me a business card with a smile that didn't quite reach his eyes. "I look forward to working with you," he said, his voice smooth like velvet.

I left the café feeling conflicted. Part of me was excited about the opportunity, but another part felt a deep unease that I couldn't shake.

I never called him. Days turned into weeks, and I continued with my life, the encounter slowly fading into the background of my memory.

It wasn't until years later, when I saw his face on the news, that the truth hit me like a cold wave. The man I had met, the charming photographer with the unsettling presence, was Rodney Alcala, the "Dating Game Killer." He had been active during the time we had crossed paths, his true nature hidden behind a facade of charm and charisma.

The realization sent a chill through me. I had unknowingly brushed shoulders with a man whose darkness was concealed beneath a veneer of normalcy. The encounter, once a forgotten memory, now haunted me, a stark reminder of how easily evil can disguise itself.

The Vampire of Sacramento

I'd never been one to believe in legends or folklore. But that all changed the summer of 1977, when I found myself caught in a nightmare that seemed far too real to be anything but the worst kind of horror.

I was just 19, living in Sacramento, and working at a small convenience store on the edge of town. The days were hot, the nights even hotter, and everything felt like it was slowly suffocating under the weight of the summer heat. I had my regular customers: the old man who liked to buy chewing gum every day, the tired mom with the screaming kids, and a few drifters who passed through town. But then, there was him.

He came in one afternoon in early June, right when the sun was at its peak. He was tall, pale, his eyes dark as if they'd never seen the light of day. His skin seemed to almost shimmer, the way a person looks when they haven't seen sunlight in too long. He didn't look like anyone I knew, not like the usual crowd at all. His clothes were simple—a tattered jacket and jeans, the kind you might see on someone who spent a lot of time on the streets—but his presence felt almost… unnatural.

He stepped up to the counter, his voice a low rasp when he spoke. "I'll take some milk. And a pack of those cigarettes."

I glanced at him as I grabbed the items, noticing the odd smell clinging to him. It was a sickly sweet odor, like something metallic mixed with a hint of decay. The kind of smell that makes your stomach twist.

"Hot day," I said, trying to make small talk, anything to break the uncomfortable silence that hung between us.

"Yeah," he replied, his voice distant, like he wasn't really paying attention to me. His eyes flickered around the store as if he was searching for something. Or someone. "A real hot one."

I handed him the items, and when our fingers brushed, I felt a sudden, inexplicable coldness. It was like a shock of ice ran through my veins. I froze for a moment, and he gave me a slight, strange smile. It wasn't warm. It wasn't kind. It was almost… predatory.

He left quickly after that, disappearing into the streets as if he were just another person passing by. But something in the back of my mind lingered. I couldn't shake the feeling that I'd met him before, though I was sure I hadn't.

It wasn't until a few weeks later, when the news hit, that I realized how wrong my instincts had been.

Richard Trenton Chase. The Vampire of Sacramento. He had been living just down the block from my store, just a few miles from my apartment, committing unspeakable horrors. He was the one they were talking about. The one who had been drinking blood, terrorizing the city, leaving a trail of death and violence. I felt a chill crawl down my spine.

But what haunted me more wasn't the news, it was the memory of him, standing in front of me, his eyes dark, his presence cold. He had been looking at me like he knew something I didn't. Something dark. Something I couldn't have known until it was far too late.

The police later revealed that he had been drawn to places like mine. Small, anonymous spaces where people come and go without notice, where no one pays close attention to the strange faces in the crowd. His prey wasn't just random. He had been watching, waiting, and I had unwittingly crossed paths with him. I don't know if I was ever truly in danger, but every time I think back on it, I wonder if he had been sizing me up, deciding whether I would be next.

For years, I couldn't shake the feeling of his cold, empty eyes on me. It was a reminder of how easily evil could slip by unnoticed, disguised as the ordinary, hiding behind the mask of an unassuming stranger. And every now and then, when the night is too quiet and the air too still, I can almost smell that sickly sweetness again, like the lingering memory of death that refuses to fade.

The Eyeball Killer

It was the fall of 1990 when I first met him. I was a 24-year-old art student, struggling to find my place in the world. My days were spent in the dimly lit corners of the Dallas Museum of Art, sketching the exhibits, trying to capture the essence of the pieces that spoke to me. It was during one of these solitary afternoons that I encountered him.

He was older than most of the patrons, with silver hair and a demeanor that suggested he had seen much in his years. He introduced himself as Charles, a former taxidermist turned art enthusiast. His knowledge of anatomy was impressive, and our conversations often delved into the intricacies of human form and structure.

Over time, our meetings became more frequent. He would sit beside me, offering insights into my sketches, his observations sharp and precise. There was something unsettling about his attention to detail, as if he was studying me more than my work. Yet, I couldn't deny the allure of his intellect and the depth of his understanding.

One evening, as the museum was closing, he invited me to his home to view his private collection. Hesitant but intrigued, I agreed. His residence was a modest house in Oak Cliff, filled with various curiosities—preserved animals, anatomical models, and shelves lined with books on human anatomy and art.

As he guided me through his collection, I noticed a peculiar pattern. Many of the preserved specimens were missing their eyes. When I inquired about it, he simply smiled and said, "The eyes are the windows to the soul. Sometimes, it's better to leave them closed."

The unease that had been building within me intensified. I made an excuse to leave, but as I turned to go, he handed me a small, wrapped package. "For your studies," he said. "A gift."

I left his home that night, the package unopened in my bag. It wasn't until I returned to my apartment that I dared to look inside. Wrapped in tissue paper was a pair of glass eyes, meticulously crafted, their lifelike appearance both beautiful and disturbing.

The next day, the news reported the discovery of a woman's body in Oak Cliff. She had been murdered, her eyes removed with surgical precision. The details matched the unsettling pattern I had noticed in Charles's collection.

I never saw him again. The museum became a place I avoided, and the memory of that night haunted me for years. The glass eyes remained in my drawer, a chilling reminder of the man who had once shared his knowledge and his darkness with me.

The Lonely Hearts Killer

It was the fall of 1953 when I first met her. I was a 28-year-old widower, recently relocated to Tulsa, Oklahoma, seeking a fresh start. The loss of my wife had left a void in my life, and I longed for companionship. One evening, while perusing the local newspaper, an advertisement caught my eye: "Lonely widow seeks kind-hearted gentleman for companionship and possibly more." The name at the bottom read "Nancy Doss."

Curious and intrigued, I penned a heartfelt letter, sharing my story and hopes for a new beginning. To my delight, I received a prompt reply. Her words were warm and inviting, filled with promises of shared dreams and mutual understanding. We exchanged letters for weeks, each correspondence deepening the connection between us. Eventually, we decided to meet in person.

Our first meeting was at a quaint café in downtown Tulsa. She was everything her letters had promised and more. Her smile was genuine, her laughter infectious, and her presence comforting. We spent hours talking, sharing stories of our lives, our losses, and our hopes for the future. By the end of the evening, I felt as though I had known her for years.

We continued to see each other regularly, and within a few months, we were married. Life with Nancy was blissful at first. She was attentive, caring, and seemed to understand me in ways no one else had. Her cooking was exceptional, and she often prepared elaborate meals that she insisted I try. I noticed she had a peculiar fondness for certain dishes, particularly those involving rich gravies and hearty stews.

However, as time passed, I began to feel unwell. At first, it was subtle—a slight fatigue, a queasy stomach, a general sense of malaise. But soon, the symptoms intensified. I became bedridden, unable to keep food down, my body weakening with each passing day. Nancy remained by my side, ever the devoted wife, tending to me with unwavering care.

One evening, as I lay in bed, struggling to stay conscious, I overheard a conversation between Nancy and a neighbor. She spoke of her previous husbands, each of whom had died under mysterious circumstances. The neighbor mentioned something about life insurance policies and how Nancy had always been the beneficiary.

That was when the truth hit me. I had been poisoned.

The next morning, I was rushed to the hospital. The doctors confirmed my worst fears—I had been poisoned, likely with arsenic. They managed to stabilize me, but the damage had been done. I never saw Nancy again. She was arrested shortly after my hospitalization and later confessed to the murders of several of her previous husbands, as well as other family members.

Her motive was chillingly simple: she sought the life insurance money and the thrill of a new romance. She had lured men through personal ads, just as she had done with me, and once they were under her spell, she poisoned them, one by one.

Nancy Doss, the "Giggling Granny," as the media dubbed her, was a master of deception. Behind her sweet smile and nurturing demeanor lay a heart as cold as ice. She had been living among us, hiding in plain sight, her true nature masked by the facade of a loving wife.

I survived, but many did not. The memory of her smile, now forever tainted by the knowledge of her crimes, haunts me to this day.

The Granny Ripper

It was a crisp evening in 2015 when I first saw her. I had recently moved to St. Petersburg, Russia, for a short-term assignment, and I was still getting accustomed to the city's eerie charm. The narrow streets, the heavy, grey skies—it all seemed like something out of a long-forgotten fairytale. But I never expected to be a part of a real-life nightmare.

I had been covering local news for weeks when the whispers about the "Granny Ripper" began to spread. The story was unsettling—an elderly woman had been arrested, accused of gruesome murders. Her name was Tamara Samsonova, and she was described as a sweet, unassuming woman, a typical grandmother. The city was still reeling from the shock. How could someone like that—someone who looked like they should be baking cookies and telling stories—commit such horrors?

One evening, after hearing more rumors from a local barmaid, I decided to take a walk through the neighborhood where Samsonova lived. It was quiet, with a faint chill in the air, as I passed rows of old buildings. Then, I saw her.

She was standing by a small convenience store, leaning against the doorframe, watching the passing cars. Her grey hair was tied up in a neat bun, and she wore a long, faded coat, typical of older women in the neighborhood. But there was something wrong. The way she watched me seemed too sharp, too calculating. It was as if she was waiting for something—or someone.

As I passed by, I felt a shiver run down my spine, and my curiosity got the better of me. I stopped just a few feet away and tried to strike up a conversation. She smiled at me, a small, pleasant smile, though it didn't quite reach her eyes. Her voice was soft, almost too soft, and she spoke with a calmness that made me uneasy.

"I see you're new here," she said. "St. Petersburg is beautiful, isn't it? But it can be lonely, especially for strangers."

I nodded, unable to hide the discomfort creeping into my chest. There was something in the way she spoke, something cold beneath the kindness.

"Yes," I replied, my voice tight. "It is... beautiful."

She gave a little laugh, the kind that might seem endearing to someone who didn't know better. "It's a lovely place. But some people don't belong here... you know?"

I froze, my instincts telling me to leave, but my feet felt heavy, rooted to the ground. Before I could say another word, she continued in a low murmur, barely audible over the hum of the street.

"Some people disappear," she said. "Sometimes it's for the best."

The air grew thick, and I found myself taking a step back. Her gaze never left me. It was then that I remembered the news reports—the ones that spoke of her arrest, the grisly details of her crimes. I felt the blood drain from my face. This was her, the woman they called the Granny Ripper. The woman whose name had become synonymous with horror.

I turned to walk away, but before I could take another step, she called out softly, "Be careful, dear. Not everyone you meet here is as they seem."

The chill in her voice lingered as I hurried back to my apartment, the image of her face burned into my mind. Later, I would learn more—how she had confessed to multiple murders, how she had lured victims with her harmless appearance, just like the many stories of her kind. But in that moment, all I knew was that I had just met a predator.

Tamara Samsonova, the "Granny Ripper," had looked like anyone's grandmother, but behind her wrinkled face and soft words lay a mind capable of horrors that most would never imagine.

I never saw her again. She was arrested shortly after, and the truth of her dark past came to light, one chilling detail after another. But every time I passed that street, I couldn't shake the feeling that she was still watching me, waiting for someone else.

Dedication

To every reader who dares to look into the darkness and understand the chilling truths that lie beneath the surface,
To those who are fascinated by the eerie whispers of the past and the terrifying reality of human nature,
This book is for you.

For the brave souls who don't shy away from the stories that make us question what we know,
For those who seek the stories of twisted minds and hidden lives,
The ones who are drawn to the shadows, yet are brave enough to confront them.

May these tales serve as a reminder of the complexity of the human experience—
the darkness that sometimes lurks in the most unexpected places,
and the monsters that may look like anyone's neighbor, family, or friend.

This book is for you: the curious, the fearless, and the willing to face the unknown.
Thank you for daring to open these pages, for walking this haunted path alongside me.
May you find a piece of yourself in these stories, and may they leave you with a thought long after the last page is turned.

Dedication

To my husband and my kids

This book is for you.

Thank you for being the light that shines through even the darkest stories I tell. While this book explores chilling encounters and the shadows of the human mind, you are the warmth that brings me back to center. Your love, laughter, and unwavering support have carried me through every chapter—both in writing and in life.

To my husband, your strength, encouragement, and belief in me never go unnoticed. You have given me the space to explore the wild corners of my imagination, while always keeping me grounded in love. You remind me every day that even in a world full of chaos, there is comfort and peace in simply being together.

To my kids, you are the brightest part of my world. Your curiosity, your fearlessness, and your endless questions inspire me more than you know. I write these stories because I believe in the power of imagination—and because one day, I hope you'll chase your passions with the same fire I feel when I write.

This book is fiction. The darkness is pretend. But the love that brought it into being? That's real. That's ours. Forever.

With all my love,

Amanda

Dedication

To my Mom and Nana

This book is dedicated to the two women who taught me the power of stories, the strength of resilience, and the importance of heart—no matter how dark the tale may be.

Mom, you have always been my fiercest supporter. Your belief in me, even when I doubted myself, gave me the courage to chase my dreams. Thank you for letting me be weird, creative, and endlessly curious. You showed me that love can be both gentle and strong—and that even the scariest stories are no match for a mother's love.

Nana, you are the foundation on which so much of who I am is built. Your wisdom, your warmth, and your unwavering grace have shaped me more than I can say. I can hear the calm in your voice and the love in your laugh. You remind me to stay humble, stay kind, and never forget where I came from—even when I'm dreaming up the wildest fiction.

This book, though filled with shadows, is rooted in the light you both gave me. You've been with me through every page I've written—whether you knew it or not. Thank you for raising me with love, patience, and just the right amount of fearlessness to write a book like this.

With all my love,
Amanda

Dedication

For My Uncle Bubber
To my Uncle Bubber—thank you for being the kind of man who never hesitated to roll up his sleeves and teach me the things that truly matter. Whether we were under the hood of a car, casting lines into the water, or just sharing laughs over the little things in life, you taught me through action and heart. You gave me memories I'll always carry with me, and your influence helped shape who I am today. This book is dedicated to you with gratitude and love—for every lesson, every moment, and every story we created together.

For My Papaw
To my Papaw—my hero, my father figure, my favorite person in the world. You may be gone from this earth, but not a day passes that I don't feel your presence guiding me. You showed me what strength looked like, what love felt like, and what it meant to be a good man. You were the steady rock in my life, the voice of reason, and the heart that kept our family grounded. This book is for you, Papaw—for all the love you gave, the wisdom you passed on, and the legacy you left behind in me. I miss you more than words can ever say, and I hope I make you proud.

Your Turn To Write

As you turn the page, I invite you to step into the narrative yourself. The stories within these pages have been written, but the next chapter is yours to create. What would your encounter with darkness look like? What sinister figure would you face, and how would you escape—or not? The blank page ahead is yours to fill with your own imagination, your own fears, and your own reflections. This is your chance to write your own tale, to explore what lurks behind closed doors in your world. So, take a deep breath, pick up your pen, and let the shadows guide you.

Made in the USA
Columbia, SC
27 May 2025